THE TREASURE HUNT

First published in hardback in Great Britain
by HarperCollins Publishers Ltd in 1996
First published in paperback by Picture Lions in 1997
This edition published by Collins Picture Books in 2003

7 9 10 8

ISBN-13: 978-0-00-715517-0
ISBN-10: 0-00-715517-4

Picture Lions and Collins Picture Books are imprints of the Children's Division,
part of HarperCollins Publishers Ltd.

Text and illustrations copyright © Nick Butterworth 1996

Visit our website at: www.harpercollins.co.uk

Printed in China

A TALE FROM PERCY'S PARK

THE TREASURE HUNT

NICK BUTTERWORTH

HarperCollins *Children's Books*

"Good morning!" said Percy the park keeper as he stepped out of his hut. In his hand, Percy was holding some posters which he had just made. He pinned one of them to his door.

"What does it say?" asked one of Percy's rabbit friends.

"Oh, I'm sorry," said Percy, and he read out loud…

I am organising a
Treasure Hunt
All those who would like to come meet at the bandstand after breakfast, tomorrow morning.
signed Percy (Me).

"I want to come," said the badger.

"So do I," said the fox. "What is it?"

"It's a game," said Percy. "One person goes off and leaves a trail of clues for the others to follow. The clues are messages, and one clue leads to the next one until you find the treasure at the end."

"I can read a bit," said the fox. He and the other animals stared at another of Percy's posters. Percy smiled as he noticed they were holding it upside down.

"I'll do drawings instead of messages," he said.

ext morning, when the animals met together, there was no sign of Percy. They thought that Percy must have forgotten, until one of the squirrels noticed something.

"Look! There's a piece of paper with a picture on it. It could be a clue."

The squirrel was right. On the paper, Percy had drawn a picture of a see-saw.

"That must be where we have to go first," said the badger.

They hurried over to the playground. Sure enough, another piece of paper had been pinned to the see-saw.

"I'll get it," said one of the mice and he scampered up the see-saw.

This time Percy had drawn
a picture of a statue.
"I know where that is," said
a rabbit. "Follow me!"
And off they went again.

By now, Percy had put nearly all his pieces of paper in place. He whistled as he walked along a favourite path at the edge of the park.

"Only two left," said Percy as he tucked one of his clues into a crack in a signpost.

He stopped for a moment and gazed over the fields which lay beyond the park.

P ercy reached into his pocket and was pleased to find some chocolate. It was chocolate money, wrapped in gold paper.

"A good job I brought a snack," said Percy, "I'm feeling quite peckish."

Slowly he ate every piece of the chocolate.

Then Percy realised
what he had done.
He had eaten
the treasure.

The animals were having great fun. Percy's trail of clues led them all over the park.

The see-saw. The statue. The tool shed. The bridge. In every place they found a picture showing them where to go next.

But now, as they searched for a clue around a signpost at the edge of the park, it didn't seem quite so easy.

"Bother," said the badger. "I can't see a clue anywhere."

The fox kept looking at the letters on the signpost. He was sure they were trying to tell him something.

"I wonder…" he muttered to himself.

Suddenly the fox announced, "This signpost is the next clue. We have to follow it."

"But it leads out of the park," said the hedgehog.

It was too late. The fox had already set off. The others looked at each other, then they followed after him.

The fox led them across a field. In the middle, there stood a tall tree which had been struck by lightning.

urther on, there was a cattle shelter.
Something was moving behind it.

"It looks like Percy," said the fox. "That must
be where he's putting the treasure."

The animals rushed towards the cattle shelter.

It wasn't Percy. But there was something there,
and the something said…

"Mooo!"

It was a young calf.

"Mmmoo!" said the calf loudly again.

The animals squealed and ran in fright towards the tree in the middle of the field.

The calf chased after them.

She wanted to play.

Lucy the calf was very friendly. When the animals had calmed down and been properly introduced, she gave them a ride across the field to the park fence.

Everyone chattered happily as they bumped along.

"We didn't find the treasure," said the fox, "but we found a friend."

Percy coughed and wiped the corner of his mouth with his handkerchief.

"And don't you think friends are better than treasure?" he said.

"Well," said the hedgehog, "I think they're about the same."

Percy smiled.

"I think you're right," he said.

Percy doesn't know that he dropped three pieces
of the treasure on his way around the park.
Can you find them?

"I was born in London in 1946 and grew up in a sweet shop in Essex. For several years I worked as a graphic designer, but in 1980 I decided to concentrate on writing and illustrating books for children.

My wife, Annette, and I have two grown-up children, Ben and Amanda, and we have put down roots in Suffolk.

I haven't recently counted how many books there are with my name on the cover but Percy the Park Keeper accounts for a good many of them. I'm reliably informed that they have sold more than four million copies worldwide. Hooray!

I didn't realise this when I invented Percy, but I can now see that he's very like my mum's dad, my grandpa. Here's a picture of him giving a ride to my mum and my brother, Mike, in his old home-made wheelbarrow!"

Nick Butterworth has presented children's stories on television, worked on a strip for *Sunday Express Magazine* and worked for various major graphic design companies. Among his books published by HarperCollins are *Thud!, QPootle5* and *Jingle Bells*, but he is best-known for his stories about Percy the Park Keeper. There are now more than 30 books about Percy, who features on video, audio tape and CD, as well as having his own television series.

Percy the Park Keeper stories can be ordered at:
www.harpercollinschildrensbooks.co.uk

Percy the park keeper is planning a treasure hunt. All his animal friends are to follow a trail of clues around the park and the first one to reach the end will find the treasure! The animals are so excited they can't wait for the hunt to begin…

This delightful story about Percy and his animal friends includes a surprise fold-out page.

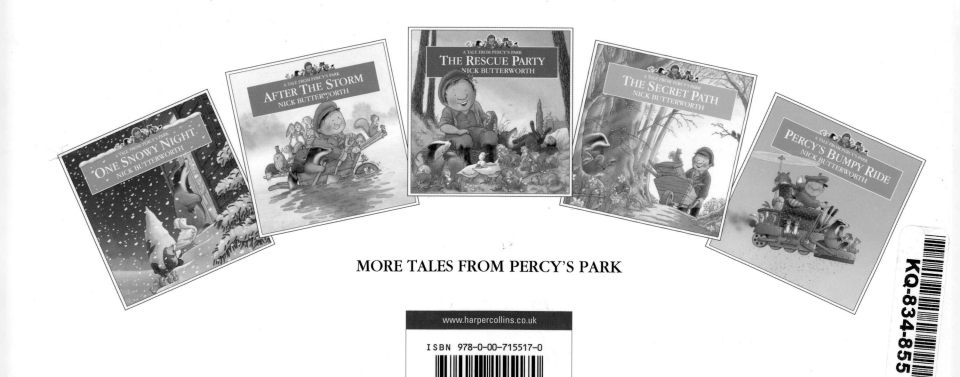

MORE TALES FROM PERCY'S PARK

www.harpercollins.co.uk

ISBN 978-0-00-715517-0

9 780007 155170

UK £5.99
CAN $9.99